Safety Superheroes:

Preventing Grandparents From Falling

Crystal Stranaghan & Izabela Bzymek

www.safetysuperheroes.com

In memory of Sara.

An example of a mother, grandmother, great-grandmother, and LIFE.

For ordering information or permissions requests, please visit the publisher's website at www.safetysuperheroes.com.

ISBN 978-0-9867103-0-8

Note for Librarians
A cataloguing record for this title is available from Library and Archives Canada at www.collectionscanada.ca/amicus/index-e.html

Printed in Canada

Message for parents, grandparents and great-grandparents

from Fabio Feldman, PhD

Each year, thousands of seniors are taken to hospitals because of injuries sustained during a simple fall. The majority of these falls happen in their own homes while performing normal daily activities such as going to the bathroom, getting up from a chair or bed, going up or down stairs, or reaching for something. Falls are often due to home hazards that are easy to overlook, but also easy to fix. This book provides a fun and engaging way of making your home safer.

In addition to making the home safer, here are other important things seniors can do to reduce their risk of having a fall or an injury due to a fall:

☑ Be active. It's important to perform at least 30 minutes of physical activity every day. Activities may include walking, exercising, gardening, dancing, and cleaning the house.

☑ Ask their doctor or pharmacist to review their medicines to reduce side-effects and interactions that may cause dizziness or drowsiness.

☑ Have their eyes checked by an eye doctor at least once a year and update their eyeglasses to maximize their vision.

☑ Wear appropriate footwear. Wear low-heeled shoes that fit well and give your feet good support. High heels, floppy slippers and shoes with slick soles can make you slip, stumble and fall.

☑ Use devices that can help keep you safe and active. If you have mobility problems, consider using a walker or cane.

☑ Eat calcium-rich foods and take calcium and Vitamin D supplements to keep bones strong.

Grandma was coming home from the hospital after recovering from a fall, and Maya, Ana and Tomer were helping Grandpa get the house ready for her return.

They had a list from the hospital of things that would make their house more safe, because no one wanted Grandma to fall again.

Tomer had a great idea. He thought making the house safer would be more fun if the kids turned themselves into Safety Superheroes!

Everyone dug through the costume box and found themselves some superhero gear.

The safety checklist said everyone should look for things on the ground that might cause someone to trip.

Ana picked up all the toys that were left on the living room floor.

Tomer picked up the magazines that had fallen on the floor and put them on the coffee table, while Maya helped Grandpa trade his floppy slippers for some indoor shoes that laced right up.

Tomer and Grandpa installed handrailings on the stairs, so Grandma would have something steady to hold onto when she climbed up to her bedroom.

Carpets that are wrinkled and have the edges rolled up are dangerous. Maya and Ana tried to smoothe out the carpet in the upstairs hallway, but it wouldn't stay flat.

Instead, they rolled the carpet up and stored it in the hallway closet so no one could trip on it.

Tomer got out the special switches that Grandpa had bought and Grandpa plugged the lamps into them.

Now lights came on like magic whenever anyone clapped their hands so that no one would ever need to walk around in the dark.

Tomer also placed the cordless phone on the nightstand so that Grandma wouldn't need to get out of bed or rush to answer the phone.

Grandma and Grandpa had a quilt on their bed that was so big it dangled right down to the floor.

That was a no-no on the safety checklist, so Maya and Ana took the too-big quilt off and put it in the laundry.

Then, they replaced it with one that stopped above the floor so no one would trip on it.

It can be difficult to reach things down low in the bathroom cupboards. Tomer and Ana moved the things Grandma used most into a basket right on the bathroom counter so they were easy to reach without bending over.

Maya put a sticky rubber mat into the bathtub so that the bottom of the tub wouldn't be so slippery, while Grandpa installed hand railings to make it easier for Grandma to get in and out of the bath.

Once the inside of the house was taken care of, everyone went outside to the front yard.

The girls wound up the garden hose onto the holder that was attached to the side of the house. Hoses are hard to see and easy to trip over when they are lying on the ground!

Grandpa and Tomer raked the rocks and bumps off of the front path so there was nothing that might cause Grandma to fall on her way into the house.

Once the Safety Superheroes had checked off every item on the Home Safety Checklist, they decided that Grandma deserved the most delicious cake in the whole world to welcome her home to her super-safe house.

Grandpa said that her favourite kind of cake was chocolate, so they got out the recipe book and went to work, mixing and measuring.

They spilled some batter, but Maya wiped it up right away so that no one would slip.

Maya went out to Grandma's garden and picked some flowers to help make the house nice and cheerful.

Ana and Tomer decorated a big WELCOME HOME banner
to hang above the table so that Grandma would know
how much everyone had missed her.

Everything was ready for when Mom and Dad brought Grandma home from the hospital.

Grandma was very happy to be home, and gave each of the superheroes a big hug to thank them for their help fixing up the house.

Everyone had a piece of chocolate cake to celebrate. It was delicious!

The Safety Superheroes had done their jobs, and they felt sure that Grandma would stay on her feet from now on!

Are you ready to take the Safety Superhero Challenge?

Name **15** things you could do to make the house
on the opposite page safer, and to prevent possible falls.

Visit us online at www.safetysuperheroes.com!

Safety Superhero Checklist
What can YOU do to keep your grandparents safe from falls?

☑ Make sure you pick up and put away all your toys, books and games so that there's nothing on the floor for people to trip over.

☑ Wear safe indoor shoes instead of floppy inside slippers, and encourage your grandparents to do the same thing!

☑ Remove any loose carpets, especially if they bunch up at the edges or won't lie flat.

☑ Make sure bathroom things are easy to reach so you don't have to bend down, or climb up to reach them.

☑ Rake up any leaves, rocks or loose gravel on porches and paths in the yard so that no one can trip over them or lose their balance.

☑ Wipe up any spills right away. You don't want anyone to slip and fall!

☑ Get your parents to help you place a cordless phone near the bed so it's easy to reach.